MW00973552

Traditions of Faith

Marta and the Manger Straw

A Christmas Tradition from Poland

Written by **Virginia Kroll**

Illustrated by **Robyn Belton**

zonder**kidz**

zonder**kidz**
The children's group
of Zondervan

www.zonderkidz.com

Marta and the Manger Straw
Copyright © 2005 by Virgina L. Kroll
Illustrations © 2005 by Robyn Belton

Requests for information should be addressed to:
Grand Rapids, Michigan 49530

Library of Congress Cataloging-in-Publication Data
data applied for

ISBN: 0-310-70994-6

All Scripture quotations, unless otherwise indicated, are taken from the HOLY
BIBLE, NEW INTERNATIONAL READER'S VERSION ®. Copyright © 1995,
1996, 1998 by International Bible Society. Used by permission of Zondervan.

All rights reserved. No part of this publication may be reproduced, stored in
a retrieval system, or transmitted in any form or by any means—electronic,
mechanical, photocopy, recording, or any other—except for brief quotations in
printed reviews, without the prior
permission of the publisher.

Zonderkidz is a trademark of Zondervan.

Editor: Amy DeVries
Art direction and design: Jody Langley

Illustrations used in this book were created using watercolor and pencil.
The body text for this book is set in Adobe Jenson.

I dedicate this book to the 732 Polish refugee children who came to New
Zealand in 1944 due to the events of the Second World War, and whose
presence has enriched our lives. My interest in this project was heightened
by the experiences of my own family sharing their lives with a refugee family
from Latvia, who became our close friends. -R.B.

Printed in China

05 06 07 08 09 /CTC/ 10 9 8 7 6 5 4 3 2 1

For my favorite Polish pastors:
Father Mark Wolska, Father Walt Szczesny, Father Ron Sajdak,
Father Rich Jedrzejewski, Father Jim Ciupek, and especially
Father Walter Grabowski, who blessed me
with the idea for this book.
—V.K.

I would like to thank Ludmila Sakowski, the Otago Polish Heritage
Trust and Pepa, my granddaughter; artist's model.
—R.B.

Author's Note

In parts of Poland at Christmas, people pull bits of straw from church manger scenes. They keep the straw in their wallets, pockets, or purses. This, they believe, will help them never be without wealth in the coming year.

No one knows how this custom got started, but it has spread to other countries. Some people believe that it has its roots in older traditions.

The idea of wealth may have started with the wise men, who brought rich gifts to the baby Jesus. Some say that the straw is special simply because Jesus is lying on it. Christians know that his spirit is alive and present among us. Only Jesus has the power to give us the richest gift of all—eternal life in heaven.

In Poland on Christmas Eve, or *Wigilia* (vee GEE lee uh), people lay fresh straw across the table and cover it with a special tablecloth. They do this in honor of Jesus' birth in a straw-filled stable.

In an old Polish countryside custom, girls and young women used straw from the table to tell their futures. If a girl reached under the tablecloth and pulled out a green stem, she would get married. A withered stem meant she would wait. A yellow one meant she would stay single.

Today, you can find Christmas garlands and mobiles made of straw, just as they were long ago. You can also find straw ornaments, such as angels, shepherds, stars, roosters, goats, and other animals.

For many Polish people the church is the center of their lives, both spiritually and socially. They make prayer an important part of each day.

In my story, Marta has the true spirit of Christmas. She shares what little wealth she has with others. And as each person is blessed, blessings come back to Marta.

Many thanks to George Fidel, Tony Smaczniak, Lucyna Dziedzic, and Stephanie Niziol Shapiro, my cousin, for help with this book.

In a poor village in Poland, Marta and her mother were leaving church after the early morning Christmas celebration.

Pastor Walter told Marta, "Take a piece of straw from the manger. Keep it with you, and you will have riches all year. And remember, Marta, there are different kinds of riches."

"Thank you, Pastor Walter," Marta said. "Merry Christmas!"

Marta pulled out a long stem of straw and slid it into the hem of her cape.

The next day, Marta walked to her grandmother's house. When she knocked, a raspy voice called, "Come in."

"Babcia (BOB chuh), you're sick!" Marta said.

"Yes, child, and I'm almost out of tea. Worse yet, I did not get to church for my piece of straw."

Marta quickly pulled out her straw and gave a bit to her grandmother.

"Bless you, child," Babcia said.

On the way home, Marta heard sobbing as she passed Plandowskis' farm.

"Why are you crying?" she asked her friend Pela (PEH luh).

"Our cow has run off," Pela said. "And now there is no milk or butter for me and my brother, Benek."

"Oh," said Marta, snapping a second bit from her straw. She folded Pela's hand around it, "Here, take this. It will bring you riches."

The next day, as Marta gathered wood for the stove, old Mrs. Wolska hobbled by. Clutching her shawl, she asked, "Dear girl, can you spare a log?"

Marta knew that she and Mamusia (mah MOO sha) were almost out of wood. But when she saw Mrs. Wolska shiver, she felt chilled herself.

"Here, take this." She gave Mrs. Wolska a fat log. "And wait!"

Marta turned up her hem and slid out the straw. *Snap!* Now Mrs. Wolska had some straw, too.

Marta slipped the now-very-short piece of straw back into her hem.

As Marta shook out the rugs, she heard a whine. She spotted two brown eyes in a mass of matted fur the color of harvested hay.

"Oh, where did you come from?" Marta asked. The sad-looking dog slowly wagged its scruffy tail.

"I don't have a bite to spare." Marta sighed. "Mamusia hasn't been to market yet. And we have little money."

There was only one thing left to do. With a silent prayer, Marta pulled the remaining bit of straw from her hem and slipped it through a snarl in the dog's ragged coat.

Just then, Mr. Rafalski's fish wagon rattled by, bouncing hard on the rutted road. Marta waved as she hurried back into the house.

After supper, Marta and Mamusia put their last log into the stove and snuggled down to sleep. As they slept, a spark spurted through a crack in the grate.

Marta and Mamusia escaped just in time. They clung to each other outside as flames gobbled up their home and everything in it.

"It's my fault," Marta sobbed. "I gave away all my manger straw, and now we are *worse* than poor!"

"No." Mamusia shook her head. "Your faith in God has made you into a loving, giving girl, Marta. And remember what Pastor Walter said. You can be rich even if you don't have money or things." She wiped away Marta's tears as they made their way to Babcia's house.

Babcia comforted them. Then Marta realized that Babcia was all better. "I am well and look at all this food my neighbors brought me. I was getting ready to celebrate with you. And did you notice the wood stacked outside? A neighbor's tree toppled in last month's storm, and he just dropped that pile off. Why, there's enough to last us all year long."

The news about Marta and Mamusia's house spread quickly through the village. Pela and Benek came by, each carrying a jug of milk. "We found our cow stuck in the muck, mooing to be milked," Pela said. "Papa wanted you to have this. He and Uncle Jan are fixing the fence so she can't escape again."

Later, Mrs. Wolska hobbled up with two beautiful
shawls for Marta and Mamusia. "My hands were so warmed
by the firewood you shared," she told Marta, "that I could
pick up my knitting again."

That evening, Marta watched the crackling fire glow in
Babcia's hearth. She heard a scratching sound. "What's that?"
she asked.

Babcia said, "It's coming from the door."

Marta bravely opened it and peered into the darkness.

"Woof."

Marta looked down. There on the stoop was the straw-colored dog with a plump, silver fish in his mouth. He wildly wagged his scruffy tail.

She smiled as the dog slurped milk from a bowl and gobbled the morsels of buttered biscuit Marta shared with him.

Later, Marta brushed the tangles from the dog's unruly fur.

"You need a name," she said. "How about 'Straw'?"

"Woof," the dog agreed.

When Marta knelt to say her prayers, Straw sat beside her with his chin on her bed. "Pastor Walter was right," she whispered. "There *are* many different kinds of riches. Thank you, God, for taking care of us."

"Woof," Straw agreed again. Then he curled into a fluffy circle at her feet and they slept snugly—and richly—through the night.

Make Your Own Straw Traditions

You might know someone of Polish descent, or perhaps you are Polish yourself.
But whether you're Polish or not, you can still enjoy some of these straw-based traditions.
(Remember to ask permission first.)

- Use real straw for your manger scene. You can get straw or hay at most garden shops, produce markets, or Christmas tree lots. It doesn't cost a lot.

- Place straw on your family's dining table underneath a tablecloth. Place a small tablecloth over the straw. During your Christmas Eve or Christmas Day meal, take turns pulling out stems of straw and comparing them. Talk about what the different lengths and colors of straw stand for. Make up your own meanings!

- Make a garland of straw. Start by tying the ends of a straw stem together. Then slip another one through the circle and tie its ends together. Keep going as you would with strips of paper and glue if you were making a paper chain. Repeat until you have a long straw chain.

- Put a piece of straw in each Christmas card you write. Include a brief explanation of the tradition.

- Make a very simple straw ornament. Cut a mini bundle of straw into even lengths. Tie a Christmas bow tightly around the middle. Double-tie the loops, and use one to hang your straw bundle on the tree.

- Make a straw star. Start with a piece of paper. Put a dot of glue, about the size of a dime, on the paper. This will be the center of the star. Cover the glue with glitter and shake off the excess. Add stems of straw, arranged like spokes of a wheel. When the glue is dry, trim off the excess paper. Add a string for hanging.

WESOŁYCH ŚWIĄT (veh SO wig shi vee ANT)!

That's "Merry Christmas" in Polish.

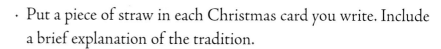